DATE DUE

Stevenson, James
 Winston, Newton, Elton
and Ed   X57617

Greenwillow
Read·alone

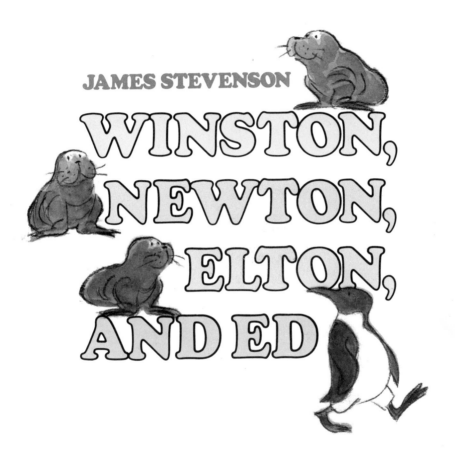

JAMES STEVENSON

WINSTON, NEWTON, ELTON, AND ED

GREENWILLOW BOOKS
A Division of William Morrow & Company, Inc., New York

10   9   8   7   6   5   4   3   2   1

Library of Congress Cataloging in Publication Data
Stevenson, James (date)   Winston, Newton, Elton, and Ed.
(Greenwillow read-alone books)
Summary: Two stories—the first featuring three
pugnacious walruses, the second, a stranded penguin.
[1. Walruses (Animals)—Fiction.   2.   Penguins—Fiction]
I.   Title. PZ7.S84748Wk [E]   77-17139
ISBN 0-688-80152-8   ISBN 0-688-84152-X lib. bdg.

CONTENTS

PLEASE DON'T FIGHT

Mrs. Waller was getting supper ready.
Winston, Newton, and Elton
were waiting around.

"This fish looks icky,"
said Newton.
He threw it away.
The fish hit Winston.

Winston threw the fish
back at Newton.

The fish bounced off Newton
and landed on Elton.

"Who is making trouble?"
said Mrs. Waller.

"Newton
and Winston,"
said Elton.

"Elton
and Newton,"
said Winston.

"Winston
and Elton,"
said Newton.

"Give me that fish,"
said Mrs. Waller.
"And don't fight."

Elton handed the fish
to his mother,
and at the same time
gave Newton a smack
with his tail.

"What is going on?"
said Mrs. Waller.
Newton said, "Elton hit me
with his tail."
Elton said, "Newton hit me
with the fish."
Newton said,
"Winston hit me with the fish."
Winston said,
"Newton hit me
with the fish first."

"Be quiet, boys,"
said Mrs. Waller,
"and behave."

Mrs. Waller gave
each one a fish.
"Eat quietly," she said,
"and don't fight."

Winston sat down
to eat his supper.
Elton sat down, too.
"Mamma! Elton is sitting
on my tail," said Winston.

"No, I'm not," said Elton.

"Winston put his tail under me."

"Move away from each other!"

said Mrs. Waller.

Elton backed away from Winston.

Elton's tail bumped Newton, and

knocked Newton's fish

into the water.

"My supper!" cried Newton.

Newton knocked Elton's fish

into the water.

"My supper!" cried Elton.

Elton grabbed Winston's fish,
and smacked Newton. "Mamma!"
said Winston. "Elton took my fish!"

"You want it?" said Elton.
He threw the fish at Winston.

It missed, and fell in the water.

Now nobody had any supper.

"That is what you get for fighting,"
said Mrs. Waller.

Elton, Newton, and Winston

sat on separate pieces of ice.

"No supper," said Winston.

"And it is all your fault,

Elton and Newton."

"Your fault," said Elton.

"You and Newton."

"Both of your faults,"

said Newton.

"And I'm starving."

It began to get
colder and darker.
Suddenly Winston said,
"Look—Mamma's got a
big new fish."
"Supper!" cried Newton.
"Hurry!" shouted Elton.

They swam to where their mother
was fixing the new fish.
"Can we have our supper?"
asked Newton.
"No," said Mrs. Waller.
"All you will do is fight."
"No, we won't," said Elton.
"I promise."

Elton climbed out of the water
and onto the ice.

"May I help you up, Newton?"
he asked.

"Thank you," said Newton.

"That would be very nice."

"My pleasure," said Elton,
pulling him up.

Then they both pulled Winston
out of the water.
"Thank you very much,"
said Winston.
"Glad to be helpful," said Newton.
"Any time," said Elton.

"Well, now," said Mrs. Waller.

"Who would like some supper?"

"After you, Elton," said Newton.

"After you, Newton," said Elton.

"I will be third," said Winston.

Then they all had supper together.

Mrs. Waller said, "See how nice

it is when you are all polite."

"But I was more polite
   than Winston," said Elton.

"No, you were not,"
   said Winston.

"I was politer than either of you,"
   said Newton.

"I was twice as polite
   as you were,"
   said Elton.

"Now don't fight,"
   said Mrs. Waller.

BEST WISHES, ED

Ed lived on a big island of ice
with Betty, Freddy, Al,
and a lot of other penguins.
Every day they had fun
throwing snowballs
and sliding on the ice.

But they always watched out
for Ernest, the big whale.
Every time he went by . . .
SPLAT!
Ed and everybody got soaked.
"Watch what you are doing!"
Betty would yell.

But Ernest swam right by.

"Ernest doesn't even notice penguins,"

said Ed.

One night when Ed was asleep,

there was a loud cracking noise.

It sounded like ice breaking.

Ed thought it was a dream.

When Ed woke up in the morning,

he found that the island of ice

had broken in half.

He was all alone

on an island of his own.

Ed's friends got smaller
and smaller
as his island drifted away.
Ed watched until he couldn't
see them anymore.

Then he walked
around his island.
There was nobody on it at all.
At last he came to his
own footprints again.

Some birds flew over.

Ed waved,

but they did not wave back.

"I guess I will be here

the rest of my life," Ed said.

At the end of the day,

he wrote

"I GIVE UP"

in big letters in the snow.

Then he went to sleep.

In the morning a tern woke him up.

"Hey," said the tern,

"did you write that thing in the snow?"

"Yes," said Ed.

"Could you write something
    for me?" asked the tern.
"I guess so," said Ed.
"What do you want?"
"Tell my friends to meet me
    at the blue iceberg,"
    said the tern.
"And sign it 'Talbot.'
    That is my name."

Talbot flew away,

and Ed wrote the message.

MEET
TALBOT
AT THE
BLUE
ICEBERG

Pretty soon, Talbot's friends
flew over and read the message.
They waved to Ed,
and Ed waved back.

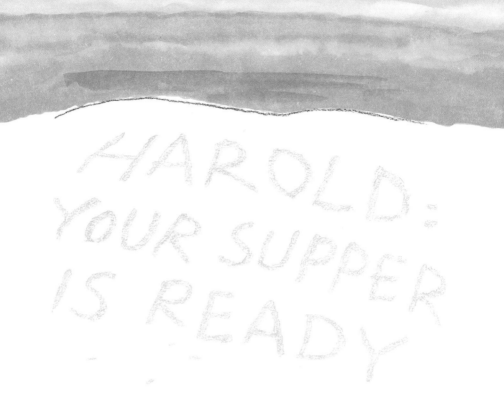

All day long, birds stopped

and asked Ed

to write messages for them.

By the end of the day,

the whole island

was covered with messages.

Ed was very tired.

DOROTHY:
MARTHA IS
LOOKING FOR
YOU

GEORGE
MARY
IS AT

Talbot landed and gave Ed a fish.
"You are doing a great job,"
  said Talbot.
"How come you look so gloomy?"
"I miss my friends
  on my old island," said Ed.
"Where is your old island?"
  asked Talbot.

"Way over there someplace,"
said Ed.

"Too bad you can't fly," said Talbot.

"You could spot it from the air."

"Well, I can't fly," said Ed.

"It's not very hard," said Talbot.

"It is for penguins," said Ed.

Talbot flew away.

"I guess I will spend the rest
of my life writing messages,"
Ed said to himself.

When Ed got up the next morning,
he found a surprise.

ED - THERE'S
A MESSAGE
FOR YOU!
FOLLOW THE ARROWS

He followed the arrows
until he came to another message.

He sat down on the X
and waited.

Suddenly there was a great SPLAT!

Ed was soaked.

It was Ernest.

"I understand you are looking
   for a ride to that island
   with all the penguins on it,"
   said Ernest.
"How did you know?" asked Ed.
"Talbot told me," said Ernest.
"Hop aboard."

"Wait one second," said Ed.

"I have to leave a message."

"Well, make it snappy,"
said Ernest.

"I have other things to do
besides give rides to penguins."

Ed quickly wrote
the message in the snow.
Then he climbed
on top of Ernest's back.

THANK YOU,
TALBOT.
BEST WISHES,
Ed

Ernest gave a couple of
big splashes with his tail,
and then they were racing
across the water.

"Ed is back!" yelled Betty.

"Hooray!" shouted Freddy and Al.

Ed slid off Ernest's back.

"Thanks a lot, Ernest," called Ed.

"That's O.K.," said Ernest.

"Just don't expect a ride every day."

"We're so glad you are back, Ed,"
  said Betty.
"We missed you a lot,"
  said Freddy and Al.
"I missed you," said Ed.

SPLAT! They were all soaked,
as Ernest swam away.

"Hey," said Betty, "he did it again!"

"Ernest doesn't notice penguins,"
said Freddy.

"Sometimes he does," said Ed.